Reading Aloud with Your Child

Research shows that reading books aloud is the single most valuable support parents can provide in helping children learn to read.

- Be a ham! The more enthusiasm you display, the more your child will enjoy the book.
- Run your finger underneath the words as you read to signal that the print carries the story.
- Leave time for examining the illustrations more closely; encourage your child to find things in the pictures.
- Invite your youngster to join in whenever there's a repeated phrase in the text.
- Link up events in the book with similar events in your child's life.
- If your child asks a question, stop and answer it. The book can be a means to learning more about your child's thoughts.

Listening to Your Child Read Aloud

The support of your attention and praise is absolutely crucial to your child's continuing efforts to learn to read.

- If your child is learning to read and asks for a word, give it immediately so that the meaning of the story is not interrupted. DO NOT ask your child to sound out the word.
- On the other hand, if your child initiates the act of sounding out, don't intervene.
- If your child is reading along and makes what is called a miscue, listen for the sense of the miscue. If the word "road" is substituted for the word "street," for instance, no meaning is lost. Don't stop the reading for a correction.
- If the miscue makes no sense (for example, "horse" for "house"), ask your child to reread the sentence because you're not sure you understand what's just been read.
- Above all else, enjoy your child's growing command of print and make sure you give lots of praise. *You are your child's first teacher—and the most important one. Praise from you is critical for further risk-taking and learning.*

—Priscilla Lynch
Ph.D., New York University
Educational Consultant

For my baby, Julianna Louise Carlson —
not a giant, but growing fast
— M.L.

For Blair and Alice Thornburgh
— R.W.A.

Library of Congress Cataloging-in-Publication Data

Leonard, Marcia.
    When the giants came to town / by Marcia Leonard ;
illustrated by R.W. Alley.
      p.   cm. — (Hello reader! Level 4)
    Summary: Stories about the giants that lived on the other side of
the mountains when Grammy was a little girl.
    ISBN 0-590-46892-8
    [1. Giants—Fiction.   2. Grandmothers—Fiction.]   I. Alley, R. W.
(Robert W.), ill. II. Title. III. Series.
PZ7.L549Whc   1994
[E]—dc20
                                       93-6225
                                          CIP
                                          AC

12 11 10 9 8 7 6 5 4 3 2 1   4 5 6 7 8 9/9
Printed in the U.S.A.   23
First Scholastic printing, November 1994

When the GIANTS Came to Town

by Marcia Leonard
Illustrated by R. W. Alley

Hello Reader!—Level 4

SCHOLASTIC INC. Cartwheel BOOKS ®
New York Toronto London Auckland Sydney

Most people think that giants
say Fee-Fi-Fo-Fum
and live in castles
at the top of beanstalks.
They think giants can be tricked by brave
little tailors and boys named Jack.
And they think that giants
are only characters in storybooks.
Not true.
Giants really do live.
Or at least they did
when my grandmother was little.
Grammy grew up in the old country.
And according to her,
the giants lived on the other side
of the mountains.

Mostly they kept to themselves.

But sometimes they'd get an urge to wander.

And they would find their way

across the mountains

to the town where Grammy lived.

These are Grammy's stories

about what happened

when the giants came to town.

Are they true? *I* think so.

Because the little girl in the stories

is Grammy herself.

THE GIANT TWINS

Once there were twin giants
named Samson and Rex.
They went hiking one fine day.
And somehow they ended up
on the wrong side of the mountains
near a small town.
"We should have turned right
at the waterfall," said Samson.
"You're wrong," said Rex.
"We should have turned left!
And now it's late and I'm thirsty."
He took a drink from his canteen.

"Not me," said Samson. "I'm hungry!
And I know for a fact
that *you* ate the last two cookies."
Rex poked through his backpack.
"There are some sunflower seeds left,"
he offered.
"Hummpf," said Samson. "Bird food."

Suddenly he spied a field of ripe melons
the townspeople had planted.
"What luck," said Samson. "Wild grapes."
He scooped them up by the handful
and popped them into his giant mouth.
In a short time, the field was empty.
"What a mess you've made," said Rex.

"Maybe if I plant something,
the ground won't look so bare and ugly."
First he used his giant comb
to make neat rows in the field.
Then he got out the sunflower seeds
and planted them in the rows.
Then he watered them with his canteen.
"*Now* can we leave?" asked Samson.
"Oh, all right," said Rex.
"Let's take the high road home."
"No," said Samson, "the low road."
And they wandered off, still arguing.

What a disaster for the townspeople!
They had planned to sell those melons
to help raise money for a new town hall.
Now they would have to wait a whole year
to grow another crop.

But overnight, something amazing happened.
The seeds sprouted, and the sunflowers
grew . . . and grew . . . and grew . . .
until they towered over the tallest trees.
All that hot summer, the sunflowers
shaded the town and kept it cool.
And when the seeds ripened,
they came down like giant hailstones.
For a week, no one could go outdoors
without an umbrella.
No one could drive
because the streets were blocked by seeds.
And all the birds grew so fat,
they could not fly.
But when it was over, the townspeople
had the richest harvest ever.
And they owed it all
to the giant twins.

THE SLEEPY GIANT

All giants love to walk.
But the champion walker of them all
was a giant named Stella.
One day, Stella decided
to walk around the world.
She walked night and day,
and she saw some wonderful sights.
She visited the pyramids in Egypt
and the ruins of an ancient city in Peru.
She slid down a glacier in Alaska
and took a shower in Niagara Falls.

But when she was nearly home,
Stella began to get tired.

In fact, she was too tired to
cross the mountains into giant land.
Her feet dragged,
her eyes closed,
and she dropped to the ground —
THUMP!

In the nearby town,
windows rattled and houses shook.
People thought it was an earthquake!
And no sooner had they recovered
from *that*, then the wind began.
WHOOOSH . . . WHOOOSH . . . WHOOOSH!
It was as regular as a clock
and twice as strong as any wind
that had whistled through town before.
Everyone hurried to the foothills to
see what it was.

And there they found Stella,
sound asleep and snoring!
WHOOOSH . . . WHOOOSH . . . WHOOOSH!
"What shall we do about this wind?"
demanded the mayor.
"Hold onto our hats," said the hatmaker.
"Fly kites," said the toymaker.
"Dry clothes," said the laundry owner.
"That's all very well," said the mayor.
"But *I* think we should do something special
with this special wind."
"We could build a windmill,"
suggested a little girl.

So that's exactly what they did.

Then they used Stella's snores
to power the windmill
to grind the sunflower seeds
to make into cooking oil
to sell to the neighboring towns
to raise enough money
to build the town hall.
Luckily, Stella didn't wake up
until the work was all done.
Then she crossed the mountains
and hurried home to dinner.

THE NOISY GIANT

Once there was a giant named Clem.
He was big and jolly
and he loved corny jokes, like
Why did the pickle close its eyes?
Because it saw the salad dressing.
And
How do you scold an elephant?
Tusk! Tusk!
Clem collected jokes and riddles
the way some people collect baseball cards.
The only problem was that
he had a very noisy laugh.
In fact, his laugh was *so* loud that
no one ever wanted
to tell him a joke.

So poor Clem had to get
joke books out of the library.
Then he'd find a spot
where no one could hear him.
And he'd read jokes and knock-knocks
and tongue twisters and limericks.
And he'd laugh and laugh and laugh.
One rainy day, Clem took his book
and crossed the mountains.
Then he settled down under his umbrella
and began to read.
Why did the chicken cross the playground?
To get to the other slide.
Why can't a bike stand on one wheel?
Because it's two tired.

At first, nobody in the nearby town
noticed Clem.
Everyone had gathered to discuss
what to do about the unfinished town hall.
Work had come to a complete stop
because it had been raining for weeks.
And the forecast called for more rain.

Then Clem began to chuckle.

"What's that?" said the mayor.

"An army on the march?" said a roofer.

"A stampede of wild elephants?"
said a carpenter.

"No," said a little girl.

"It's a giant chuckling."

Clem's chuckle turned into a guffaw.

Then the guffaw turned into a laugh.

The noise was so loud that

it made dogs howl and babies cry.

It made trees drop their leaves

and ducks shed their feathers.

And wonder of wonders,

it made the heavy rain clouds

break into little bits

and blow away.

So when Clem finished his book

and went home,

the builders could finally finish

the town hall.

THE VAIN GIANT

Ruby was a very vain giant.
She was convinced that she was
the most beautiful giant in the land.
And she liked nothing better
than to stare at her own reflection.
But none of her mirrors
ever seemed quite big enough.
So one day she set out to find
a large pond.
She wanted to sit on the bank
and admire herself in the still water.

She crossed the mountains.
Then she wandered into town
just as the mayor was finishing
a very long speech to dedicate
the new town hall.

Now it must be said
that Ruby was as silly as she was vain.
She looked at the balloons,
the ribbons, and the brass band.
She looked at the brand-new town hall.
"A present for me!" she said.
"And it isn't even my birthday!
But I accept, of course."
She lifted off the top
of the town hall clock tower.
Then she put it on her head.
"Thank you for the lovely hat!
I must see what I look like," she said.
And she hurried off to the pond.
"Wait!" shouted the mayor.
"Come back with our tower!"
shouted the townspeople.

They ran after Ruby.
But even the fastest runners
could not keep up with her.
So they sat down to wait — and hope.
Minutes passed.
Hours passed.
Finally Ruby returned.
"It *is* a lovely hat," she said.
"And I *do* look beautiful in it.
But I'm afraid it is too heavy."

She placed the top of the tower
back on the town hall.
Then she went home to her mirrors.
The townspeople were very happy
to have the top of their tower back.
The mayor finished his speech.
The band played.
And the town hall was officially opened.
But there was one small problem.
Ruby had put the top of the tower
back on upside down!

So from then on, the townspeople
had to stand on their heads
to see what time it was.

THE HELPFUL GIANT

osco was a giant
with good intentions.
But whenever he tried to be helpful,
something usually went wrong.
One day he decided to help
his mother make soup.
But he dropped the pepper,
which made him sneeze,
which scared the cat,
which knocked over a vase,
which broke into a hundred pieces,
which made his mother yell.

So Rosco went for a walk until
things calmed down at home.
As he crossed the mountains,
he saw a funny sight.
There was a miniature town
with a brand-new town hall.
But the top of the town hall tower
was on upside down!
"Clearly, these people need my help,"
said Rosco.

He turned the top of the tower
the right way around
and carefully set it down in place.
When the townspeople saw
what he had done,
they all cheered.
"Hip, hip hooray!
Hooray for the helpful giant!"

How nice, thought Rosco.
I wonder what else I can do to help.

He decided that the town hall
could use some shade.
So he uprooted big trees
from all over town
and replanted them around the hall.
He decided that a herd of cows
needed greener grass to eat.
So he took them from their pasture
and put them down in the park.

He decided that the town's only bus
needed washing.
So he dunked it in the duck pond.
And he decided that the children
needed a swimming pool.
So he dug a big, wide hole
in an empty field.

By this time, the townspeople
were all yelling at him.
But Rosco thought
they were cheering for him again!
"You don't have to thank me," he said.
"I'm just glad I could help."

And he left the poor townspeople
to weep for their shade trees,
round up the cows,
dry out the bus,
and stare at the big, wide hole
in the empty field.

THE GIANT BABY

Once there was a giant baby
whose name was Lily.
What she liked was
eating and sleeping and crawling
and being cuddled.
What she didn't like was
being alone.
One day Lily's daddy put her
in the backpack and took her
for a walk across the mountains.
By the time they reached
the other side,
they were both tired.

So they had a little nap.
But Lily woke up first
and went for a crawl.
At first she was quite happy.

But when she reached the nearby town,
she suddenly realized
that her daddy wasn't with her.
Then she started to cry.
Her first shriek brought
all the mothers running.
Her second brought the fathers.
Her third brought everyone else,
including the mayor from his bath.
"Why is that baby crying?"
he demanded.
"Maybe she's thirsty," said a mother.
So the farmers brought Lily some milk.
But she kept on crying.
"Maybe she's tired," said a father.
So the choir sang lullabies to Lily.
But she kept on crying.
Then the grandmothers
made her some porridge.
And the grandfathers told her stories.

But Lily just kept crying.
She cried so hard and so long,
her tears made a river
that flowed down the street.

"We've tried everything,"
shouted the mayor.
"What does this baby want?"
"I think she wants her daddy,"
said a little girl.
"And here he comes now!"
Lily's father scooped her up
and gave her a big hug.
"Don't cry. Daddy's here," he said.
Lily stopped crying — and smiled!
The townspeople smiled.
"Look!" said the little girl.
"The baby's tears filled up the hole."
Sure enough, the river of tears
had flowed into the big, wide hole
the helpful giant had dug.
The townspeople had a swimming pool!
And no one seemed to mind
that the water was a little bit salty.

THE FORGETFUL GIANT

Once there was a giant so forgetful,
he often forgot his own name —
which happened to be Max.
One day Max set off for the store.
He had made a shopping list
so he would remember what to buy.
And as he walked along,
he read it out loud:
"Muffins, butter, strawberry jam,
lettuce, mustard, thin-sliced ham.
Pickles, carrots, Cheddar cheese,
ginger snaps, and herbal teas."
That sounds like lunch, thought Max.

He forgot he was going to the store
and hurried home to eat.
But when he reached the house,
the door was locked.
Perhaps I've gone for a walk,
thought Max.
He forgot about lunch
and set off across the mountains.
By the time he reached
the little town on the other side,
he was hot and tired.

"Yes, I can say quite definitely
that I went for a walk," said Max.
He patted his brow with his hankie
but forgot to return it to his pocket.
So the hankie fell on the playground
and covered twelve kids.

He pulled open his collar
but forgot to unbutton it first.
So the top button popped off
and rolled down Main Street.

Then he took off his shoes and socks
and cooled his feet in the pond.
But he was still hot.
So he reached in his pocket
for his hankie
and found his grocery list instead.
"I must go shopping," he said.
He forgot about his socks,
put on his shoes, and set off at once.
This time he actually reached the store.
And as for the things he left behind,
the townspeople put them to good use.
The hankie made a great tent.
And the socks made fine blankets —
once they'd been given a scrubbing.

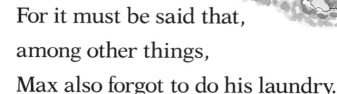

For it must be said that,
among other things,
Max also forgot to do his laundry.

Well, that's the last
of Grammy's giant tales.
I hope you liked them.
"But, wait a minute," you say.
"What happened to the giant button —
the one Max lost
in the last story?"
That's easy.
My grammy and her dad
made it into a table.
If you don't believe me,
go into Grammy's dining room
and peek under the tablecloth.
You can see it for yourself.